WATTY

THE BROONS AND OOR WULLIE 1936-1996

FROM the first publication in March 1936, Oor Wullie and The Broons have appeared every week in "The Sunday Post".

The characters, as can be seen in the following pages, have changed slightly, but they have never aged. Generations have followed the ploys of the characters, Scotland's best-loved fowk.

During the years of World War II, "The Sunday Post" went out to the lads and lassies serving in the Armed Forces at home and abroad. Oor Wullie and The Broons quickly became great favourites with the Allied troops in every theatre of war.

The original illustrator, Dudley D. Watkins, continued to produce both strips until his sudden death on August 20th, 1969. His illustrations, reprinted in this book, are regarded as classics in the characterisation of Scottish life.

Today, as in the early days, the weekly stories are created by an in-house editorial team and brought to life by the illustrator, currently Ken H. Harrison.

It is a mark of the ageless qualities of the characters, that Wullie and the family from No. 10 Glebe Street, are as popular as ever with the readers of today's "Sunday Post".

CONTENTS

The endpapers (pages 2/3 and 142/143) were originally drawn for use as jigsaw puzzles.

ISBN 085116 633 4

Printed and published in Great Britain by D. C. Thomson & Co., Ltd., 185 Fleet Street, London EC4A 2HS © D. C. Thomson & Co., Ltd., 1996

THE SUNDAY POST. MARCH 8, 1936.

The Sunday Post

NO. 1593.

PRINTED AND PUBLISHED IN GLASGOW EVERY SUNDAY MORNING.

[REGISTERED AT THE GENERAL POST OFFICE AS A NEWSPAPER.]

SUNDAY, MARCH 8, 1936.

Morning Special

PRICE TWOPENCE.

EUROPE ALARMED

VIEWS OF COLOGNE AND FRANKFURT IN THE DEMILITARISED RHINELAND ZONE, WHICH COMPRISES THE LEFT BANK OF THE RHINE, AND A 50-KILOMETRE STRIP OF THE RIGHT BANK. THE ZONE INCLUDES AIX-LA-CHAPELLE, TRIER, THE ARMAMENTS CITY OF ESSEN, AND THE SAAR.

France Demands Evacuation Of The Rhine

AND RUSHES SOLDIERS TO FRONTIER

Every Capital in Europe is seething with excitement following Hitler's denunciation of the Locarno Treaty, and the dramatic march of German troops into the demilitarised Rhineland zone.

France is greatly perturbed, and early this morning the news was received from Paris that the French Government intends to insist on the evacuation of German troops from the demilitarised zone, and will demand the support of Great Britain, Italy, and Belgium.

M. Flandin intends to call a meeting of the Powers signatory to the Locarno Treaty in Paris to-morrow evening to fix a common attitude for Geneva.

The French Government considers it can count on British support after Mr Eden's statement in the House of Commons.

FRENCH TROOPS RE-OCCUPY RHINE BRIDGE

To-day French troops are being rushed to man frontier fortifications and intermediate sections. All army leave has been stopped, and soldiers have been recalled from leave.

The Kehl Bridge over the Rhine near Strasbourg, which was evacuated by the French under the Locarno agreement, has now been occupied by French troops.

German troops had already reached the Rhine at this point. To-day German and French soldiers will be facing each other in this

The French troops holding the Kehl Bridgehead will, however, be hemmed in by the German troops which reached the Rhine yesterday.

Mr Anthony Eden, after seeing French, Belgian, and Italian Ambassadors in London, hurried to Chequers, and had a long talk with Baldwin.

The Cabinet will discuss the situation at a special meeting called Sunday. To-night in well-informed diplomatic circles it is stated Ministers take the view that the situation is very serious, but there is no need for panic.

SOLDIERS FETED IN

Better a G... in th...

Britain Paramou... Meik on

Alarming as the German action appears at first sight a calm and impartial examination reveals that, far from imperilling further the already strained situation in Europe, a position has arisen where, with continued understanding and good will, the cause of lasting peace may be strengthening of the League may be served

In Britain the move has been taken calmly, as it has long been realised that, as the Treaty of Versailles has proved a failure, it is better to have a Germany out in the open than a Germany smouldering behind a screen.

Now that Germany has acted, opinion is gaining ground that what she has done against the Treaty is balanced by her straightforward offer of a 25-year non-aggression pact and a return to the League.

This offer is at the moment discounted by France and Russia, but from Germany's point of view, it is the only possible answer Hitler could make to the Franco-Russian pact.

However nervous France is, the League will have to consider the ques...

FRENCH CRITICISM OF BRITAIN

A remarkable comment is made by Dr Pech... of the Army Committee of the Chamber, who, aft... tude of Britain towards Italy, says:—

We may lose both Locarno and Stresa

Army may have to take a stand on two fr...

Army will not be ready for six months.

In Rome Germany's offer to re-enter the League... The first impression is one of satisfaction. It... League is too much under the domination of Great that the return of Germany will provide a useful...

In Vienna Hitler's speech caused the grave... A great slump set in immediately...

MARCH 8th, 1936

"The Sunday Post" of the day leads with the headline "EUROPE ALARMED". Eighteen years after the end of the so-called Great War (1914-1918), Germany is moving troops back into the Rhineland. German and French soldiers face each other across the river Rhine as alarm bells ring across Europe.

On the home front, "The Sunday Post" is offering eight lucky readers the chance to win a free trip aboard the pride of the river Clyde, the new luxury liner QUEEN MARY.

Also on March 8th, Post sports reporters tell of 41,663 spectators packing into Pittodrie to see Rangers defeat Aberdeen 1-0 in the Scottish Cup. (Rangers go on to win the cup this season, Celtic taking the honours in the league race.) In England Wolves go down 1-0 to Blackburn Rovers while Chelsea lose 2-1 at home to Sheffield Wednesday.

There is also this Sunday of March 8th, 1936, a new addition to "The Sunday Post", a special FUN SECTION 8-page pull-out. It includes a big cartoon illustration of the soccer at Auchentogle between Dubbin Alley Celtic and Whigmaleerie Rangers. There are jokes from Merry Mac, Funland puzzles and cartoon strips featuring, amongst others, Wishbone Wuzzy, Silas Snatcher the Truant Catcher and Barnacle Bill. Page one of this new FUN SECTION features a wee lad in dungarees called OOR WULLIE, while on page five, THE BROONS OF GLEBE STREET take a bow.

OOR WULLIE and THE BROONS are destined to become household names.

Thomas Rennie, hotelkeeper, Laurencekirk, had come to Aberdeen to see the match, and was waiting for friends at the...

This caused astonishment. It is generally felt that the domination of Great Britain and France, and...

OOR WULLIE 1936-1939

The very first issue. Jings! Crivvens! Help ma Bob! How things have changed!
There's no way Wullie would get away with this anti-social behaviour today.

The Sunday Post 8th March 1936

The Broons appear for the first time. You will see in the pages to follow how quickly the characters evolve. Barely recognisable here, it is only a matter of weeks before the characters are firmly established.

The Sunday Post 8th March 1936

THE BROONS 1936-1939

The original Broons title, naming all the members of the Broon clan, was used every week until November 6th, 1938, by which time the characters had evolved to such an extent that they were unrecognisable compared to the original illustrations.

Granpaw Broon didn't make his debut until September 6th, 1936, and it was November 13, 1938, before he was added to the characters in the title illustration. Even then he was only shown in a photograph on the wall.

The next significantly altered title illustration appeared on Sunday, 29th October, 1939, when Hen and Joe Broon were shown in army uniform. Granpaw

Broon remained remote in his picture frame, but sported a gas mask! Hen and Joe in fact remained in uniform until March 10th, 1946. To a large extent they also disappeared from the stories on February 7th, 1943, while on active service.

The Sunday Post 4th July 1937

9

OOR WULLIE 1936-1939

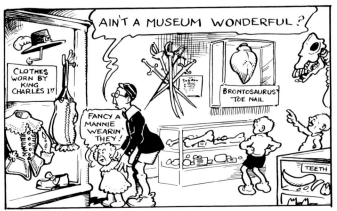

The Sunday Post 22nd August 1937

OOR WULLIE 1936-1939

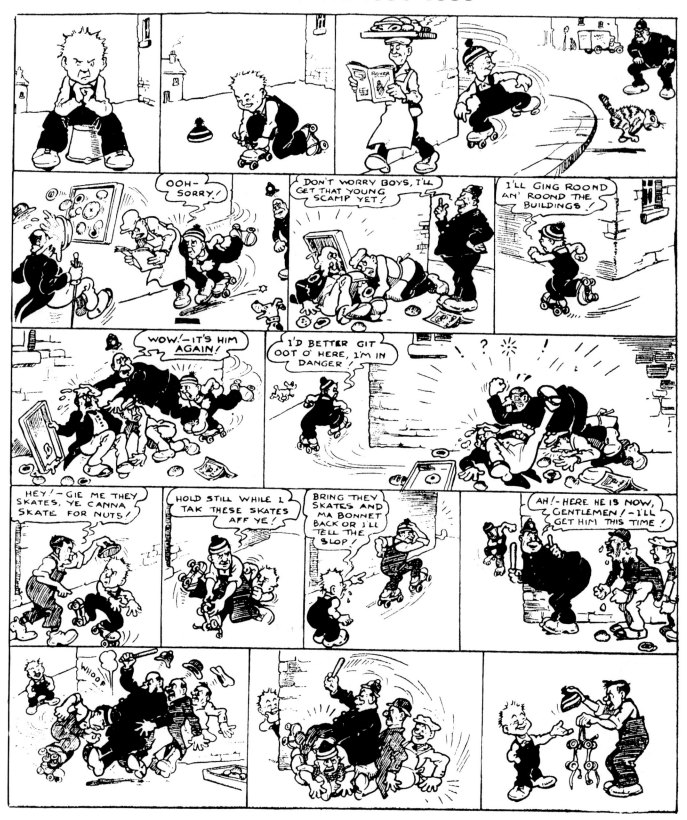

Here we see the title page of the eight-page "Fun Section" newspaper pull-out.

By April 1941, this was reduced to four pages, due to the wartime paper shortage. The many features had been trimmed to include only Merry Mac's jokes, Funland puzzles, Nero and Zero, Nosey Parker and, of course, Oor Wullie and The Broons.

This line-up was to continue until February 15th, 1976.

The Sunday Post 23rd January 1938

OOR WULLIE 1936-1939

The Sunday Post 30th January 1938

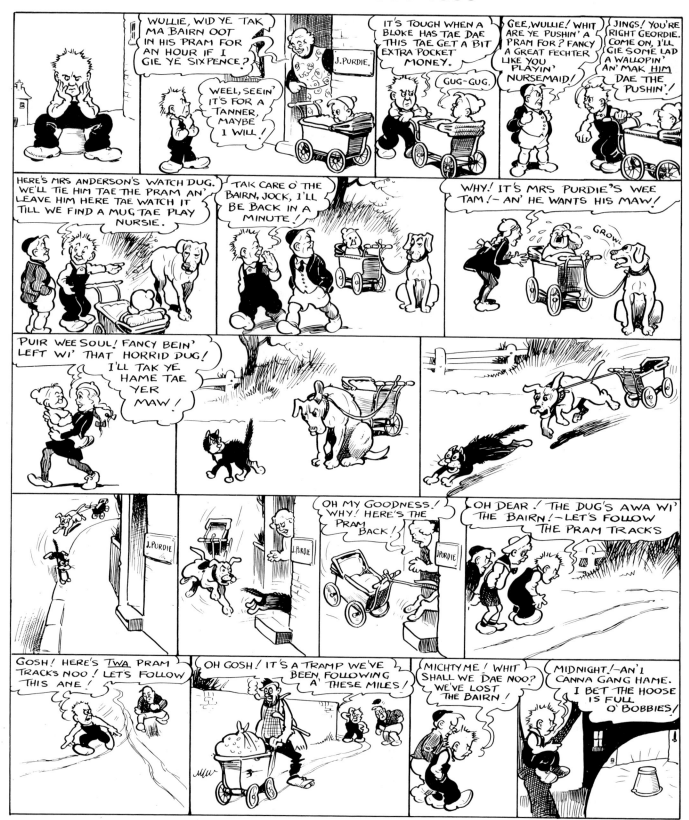

OOR WULLIE 1936-1939

Just as Wullie would have landed in serious trouble with his debut antics today,
a fireworks stunt like this would land today's editorial team right in it beside him!

The Empire Exhibition (Scotland) of 1938 was held in Glasgow's Bellahouston Park and ran from the 3rd of May to the 29th of October. Its aim was to promote the British Empire and highlight the United Kingdom's, particularly Scotland's, development and resources.

The Sunday Post 3rd July 1938

B

OOR WULLIE 1936-1939

The Sunday Post 23rd July 1939

SCOTLAND'S FAVOURITE — OOR WULLIE IN A BOOK

The Sunday Post 6th October 1940

THE STORY OF A GRAND NEW PICTURE BOOK

The Sunday Post 5th November 1939

THE WAR YEARS 1939-45
THE HOME FRONT

THE SUNDAY POST, SEPTEMBER 3, 1939.

The Sunday Post

PRINTED AND PUBLISHED IN GLASGOW EVERY SUNDAY MORNING

NO. 1775. [REGISTERED AT THE GENERAL POST OFFICE AS A NEWSPAPER]

SUNDAY, SEPTEMBER 3, 1939.

RADIO—PAGE 3   PRICE TWOPENCE.

Morning Special

GERMAN FORCES WITHDRAW

PREMIER'S STATEMENT IN COMMONS

Time Limit To Germany Being Considered

Last night Britain and France still awaited Hitler's reply to the final warning that the guarantee of Poland will become operative unless German troops are withdrawn from Polish territory.

Before a packed House of Commons last night the Premier made these points:—

If the German Government would withdraw from Polish territory H.M. Government would be willing to regard position as the same as it was before the invasion.

Sir Nevile Henderson was received by Herr Von Ribbentrop at half-past nine last night, and Ribbentrop said he would have to deliver our warning message to the German Chancellor.

While appreciating the efforts of the Italian Government he found it impossible to take part in a conference when Poland was being subjected to invasion. (Loud and prolonged cheers.)

H.M. Government would, as stated yesterday, be bound to take action unless the German forces were withdrawn from Polish territory. (Cries of "When?")

They were in communication with the French Government as to the limit of time within which it would be necessary to know whether the German Government would be prepared to retire.

The situation would still be open to discussion between German and Polish Governments on understanding that settlement safeguarded vital interests of Poland and was secured by international guarantee.

If the German and Polish Governments wished other Governments to be associated with them in the discussions H.M. Government would be prepared to co-operate.

ARMED FORCES BILL

The House of Commons considered the National Service (Armed Forces) Bill. Mr Ernest Brown, Minister of Labour, announced that all men between the ages of 18 and 41 must register and would be medically examined and then called upon when required.

Mr Brown said it was not intended at the outset that any considerable number of men should be called up. Steps would be taken to ensure that the man-power essential to industry would not be disturbed.

The introduction of the Bill was carried by 340 votes to 7 and was read a second time without a division.

A meeting of the Cabinet was held yesterday afternoon and delayed Chamberlain's attendance at the Commons.

The Commons will meet again at noon to-day.

MUST
TO THE RESCUE

What—lost already, so soon on Evacuation day? But the baby had a fine new label, the policeman a fine new helmet, and between them the problem was soon solved. (Stories of the Evacuation on page 5.)

ALL MEN BETWEEN 18 AND 41 TO REGISTER

SEPTEMBER 3rd, 1939

September 3rd, 1939. Germany has invaded Poland, Britain declares war and the world is plunged into six years of horror. At number 10 Glebe Street, The Broons prepare to play their part in the great armed struggle.

"The Sunday Post" (issue dated 10.3.39, see page 47) sees great activity in the house. Hen and Joe are already in uniform and even Granpaw Broon is cycling off to offer his services to King and country . . .

The Sunday Post 17th September 1939

The Sunday Post 15th October 1939

The Sunday Post 12th November 1939

OOR WULLIE 1939-1945

OOR WULLIE 1939-1945

The Sunday Post 15th March 1942

The Sunday Post 24th May 1942

OOR WULLIE 1939-1945

The Sunday Post 20th September 1942

OOR WULLIE 1939-1945

The Sunday Post 13th December 1942

The Sunday Post 17th October 1943

The Sunday Post 30th January 1944

OOR WULLIE 1939-1945

WHIT ARE YE BLAWIN' YER HAUNDS FOR?

CLASS 2A

THERE'S A NEW TEACHER AN' HE'S AN AULD BLOKE AN' AWFY ILL TEMPERED — HE JUIST GAVE ME SIX WI' THE STRAP!

OH CRIVVENS! AN' I'M LATE!

SO! TRYIN' TO SNEAK INTO CLASS WITHOUT ME SEEIN' YE, EH? COME HERE YOU!

AN' WHAT D'YE MEAN BY COMIN' IN LATE!

MA MITHER SENT ME A MESSAGE FOR SPLIT PEAS, AN' — ER — I HAD TAE SPLIT THEM!

OH, IS THAT SO? WELL, SINCE YOU'RE SO SMART, WHAT'S 9 TIMES 9?

OH-ER, AN AWFY LOT—MAYBE ABOOT TWA HUNDER!

AN' WHERE IS THE BAY OF BISCAY?

I-I TH-THINK IT'S ALANG SAUCHIEHALL STREET SOME PLACE!

FOLLOW ME, BOY!

SLAP WALLOP WOW OUCH OOH

THAT NIGHT I'VE GOT A PLAN TAE GIE WIR NEW TEACHER A FRICHT — FIRST I'LL MAK' MASEL' A PAIR O' LANG LEGS!

COULD I BORROW ANE O' YER AULD UNIFORMS, P.C. MURDOCH?

BE CAREFU' WI' IT!

THANKS A LOT!

NEXT MORNING

AT SCHOOL SO! YOU'VE BEEN THRASHING MY SON WULLIE, EH?

I'M GOING TAE GIVE YOU WHIT YOU GAVE HIM! HAUD OOT YER HAND!

WHAT— IN FRONT OF THE CLASS?

15—16—17 — I'LL TEACH YOU A LESSON!

HOORAY WHOOPEE

HELP! HELP! STOP—OOH!

TINGLE

OH THANKS, BOBBY! THAT WIS GREAT!

DON'T MENTION IT, IT WIS A PLEASURE!

HEY, POLISMAN! YER BREEKS ARE FA'IN' DOON!

JINGS! IT'S NO' A POLIS AT A'— IT'S OOR WULLIE ON STILTS!

WHAT!!

NEXT DAY YE'LL NO' GET A LICKIN' EFTER A' WULLIE! YON TEACHER'S LEFT THE TOON AN' WINNA BE BACK!

The Sunday Post 28th January 1945

The Sunday Post 29th April 1945

The Sunday Post 13th May 1945

COVER

Pictured here are all the "Broons" and "Oor Wullie" annual covers from the very first "Broons" book, published in 1939, to the present day "Oor Wullie" book. Between 1943 and 1946, no "Broons" or "Oor Wullie" books were printed due to the paper shortage in Britain in World War II. "The Broons" reappeared in book form in 1947 and, alongside "Oor Wullie", have been published bi-annually ever since.

1939	1940	1941	1942	1947	1948
1949	1950	1951	1952	1953	1954
1955	1956	1957	1958	1959	1960
1961	1962	1963	1964	1965	1966

STORY

1967 · 1968 · 1969 · 1970 · 1971 · 1972
1973 · 1974 · 1975 · 1976 · 1977 · 1978
1979 · 1980 · 1981 · 1982 · 1983 · 1984
1985 · 1986 · 1987 · 1988 · 1989 · 1990
1991 · 1992 · 1993 · 1994 · 1995 · 1996

THE WAYS AND WILES O' OOR WULLIE

*F*AIR fa' your rosy-cheekit face,
  Your muckle buits, wi' broken lace,
Although you're always in disgrace,
    An' get your spanks,
In all our hearts ye have your place —
    Despite your pranks.

Your towsy heid, your dungarees,
Your wee snub nose, your dirty knees
Your knack o' seeming tae displease
    Your Ma an' Pa.
We dinna care a tuppenny sneeze —
    We think you're braw.

You're wee, an' nae twa ways aboot it,
You're wise, wi' very few tae doot it,
You're wild, there's nane that wad dispute it,
    Around the toon.
But maist o a' ye are reputit —
    "A lauchin' loon."

Weel-kent, weel-liked, you're aye the same,
Tae Scots abroad and Scots at hame.
North, south, east, west, your weel-won fame
    Shall never sully.
We'll aye salute that couthie name —
    Oor Wullie.

DUDLEY D. WATKINS

Adapted from The Oor Wullie Annual 1954

POST WAR AND BEYOND 1945-59

THE SUNDAY POST, JUNE 7, 1953.

The Sunday Post

No. 2493.

REGISTERED AT THE GENERAL POST OFFICE AS A NEWSPAPER.

PRINTED AND PUBLISHED EVERY SUNDAY MORNING.

SUNDAY, JUNE 7, 1953.

Radio and TV—Page 4

PRICE 2½d.

Morning Special

ARISE, SIR JOHN AND SIR EDMUND!

EVEREST: THE QUEEN HONOURS HER HEROES

AT LONG LAST, IT WAS SIR GORDON'S DAY

The Queen shakes hands with Gordon Richards at Epsom yesterday. Gordon put Pinza first past the post four lengths ahead of the Queen's horse, Aureole.

And Epsom Looked SO Different!

MR EDMUND HILLARY, who, with Sherpa Tensing, conquered Mount Everest, and Colonel John Hunt, leader of the expedition, are to be knighted by the Queen. This was announced last night from 10 Downing Street.

The statement said the Queen approved that the honour of knighthood be conferred upon Colonel Hunt and that Mr Hillary be appointed a Knight Commander of the Order of the British Empire.

"It is also Her Majesty's desire to recognise the achievement of Sherpa Tensing. Since he is not a British subject, this requires consultation, and no immediate announcement can be made."

The British Government is already in consultation with the Government of Nepal concerning the honour to Sherpa Tensing.

Mrs Hunt, speaking on the phone from her home, told a reporter, "I hardly know what to say. I am delighted.

"I think I know what my husband's reaction will be. He will look upon it as an honour to the whole expedition."

Mrs Hunt, who is 39, is a former Wimbledon tennis player. She is also well-known as a Himalayan climber. She married Colonel Hunt in 1936 and still has a practical interest in climbing.

Commenting on the award to Mr Hillary, the Prime M[...] Zealand [...]

EVEREST LEADER MAY VISIT DUNDEE

JUNE 7th, 1953

The post-war years saw THE BROONS and OOR WULLIE firmly established as household names. Scriptwriters, many returning from war service, and artist were working in practised harmony and it is in this period that many aficionados consider the strips to be at their peak.

Britain slowly recovers from the horrors of World War II and OOR WULLIE and THE BROONS continue to entertain the millions of readers, as their popularity goes from strength to strength.

A new monarch is on the British throne and a new hero is on the summit of Mount Everest.

WHAT a[...]
was!
[...] Derby it

Gordon Richards, 49-year-old Knight of the Turf, yesterday [...]

Of the race he said [...] had an easi[...]

OOR WULLIE 1945-1959

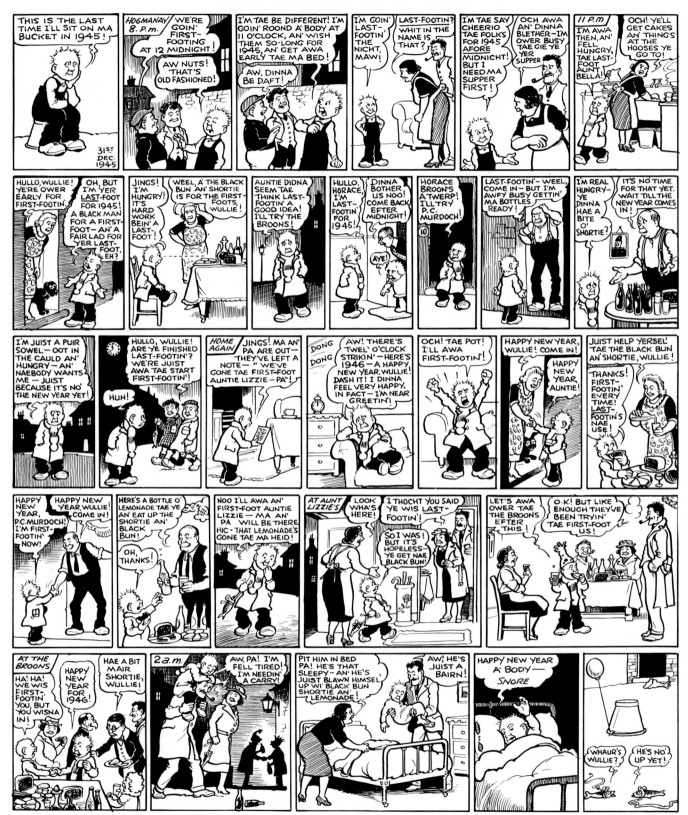

OOR WULLIE 1945-1959

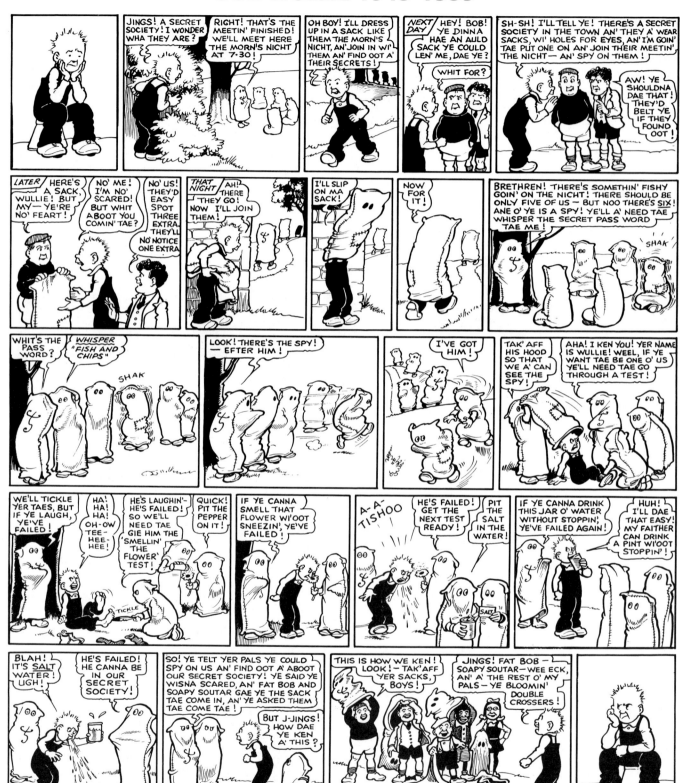

OOR WULLIE 1945-1959

OOR WULLIE 1945-1959

The Sunday Post 31st December 1950

The Sunday Post 20th May 1951

The Sunday Post 10th September 1950

OOR WULLIE 1945-1959

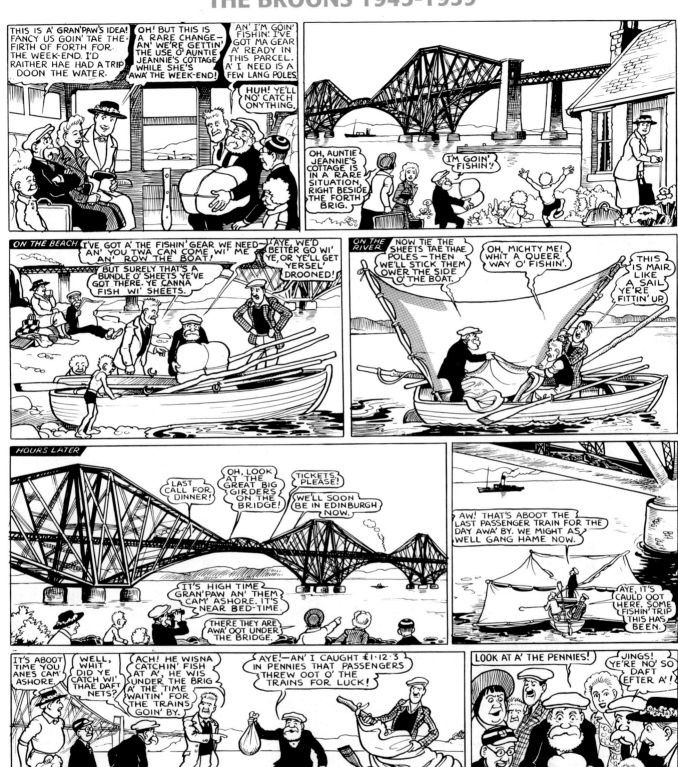

The Sunday Post 8th July 1951

OOR WULLIE 1945-1959

The Sunday Post 6th May 1951

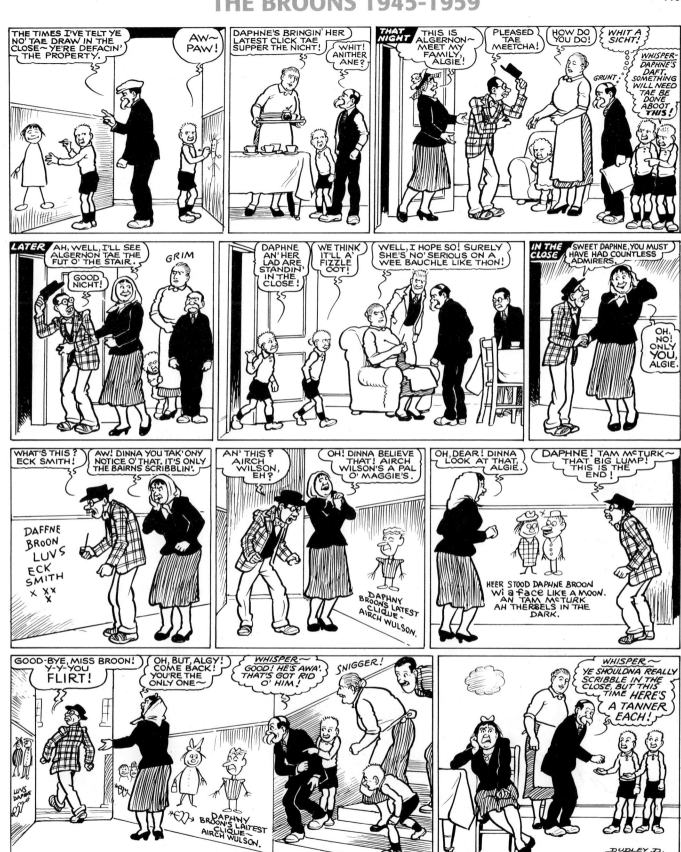

The Sunday Post 31st May 1953

OOR WULLIE 1945-1959

The Sunday Post 12th August 1956

The Nobility Broons

In days of yore, long, long ago,
The Broons were famous Scots.
Broon Castle was the family seat.
Of titles they had lots.

Duke Paw and Duchess Maw oft-times
  Would stroll in the estates,
Or take a drive, by coach and four,
  Outside the castle gates.

Sir Henry and Sir Joseph Broon
  Each hunted, fished and shot.
Sir Horace, scribbling with his quill
  Would tally what they'd got.

The Lady Mag and Lady Daph
  Most nights were kept "reel" busy,
Birlin' at some grand Clan Ball
  Till baith of them were dizzy.

The Honourable Twins and Bairn —
  A threesome full of fun!
Each day, they had their tutor and
  Their nanny on the run.

In Auld Yins' Castle, doon the road,
  Lived First-Duke Gran'paw B.
Of a' the gentry in the land,
  The noblest O.A.P.!

Now fancy that, Ye wouldna think
Such grandeur could be true?
It ISN'T! — NO, The Broons aye were
Plain folk, like me and you.

Adapted from The Broons Annual 1967

The Sunday Post, July 20, 1969.

The Sunday Post

Morning Special

No. 3334

PRINTED AND PUBLISHED EVERY SUNDAY MORNING.

[REGISTERED AT THE GENERAL POST OFFICE AS A NEWSPAPER.]

SUNDAY, JULY 20, 1969.

TV and Radio — Page 12.

Price 7d.

APOLLO 11 IN ORBIT ROUND THE MOON

Ready For Landing Tonight

APOLLO 11 is in moon orbit and all is set for tonight's landing.

The engine firing to make it brake took place behind the moon and out of radio contact with earth yesterday evening.

A great stillness descended on the Houston mission control during the 45 minutes the spacecraft was on the other side.

Commander Neil Armstrong later reported the braking burn of the main engine was "like perfect."

Armstrong is due to set foot on the moon just after seven to-morrow morning.

But with things going so well this may be advanced by a few hours.

As they made their first sweep close to the moon, Armstrong told ground control the pock-marked surface looked very much like the pictures and maps brought back to Earth two months ago by Apollo 10.

"But there's no substitute for the real thing," he added.

He said it was too dark to get a proper look at the site selected for tonight's landing.

"At the terminator (the line between day and night) it's ash and grey.

"As you get farther away from the terminator it gets to be a light grey and, as you get closer to the sub-solar point, you can definitely see browns and tans on the ground."

For Posterity

In Houston, spacecraft communicator Bruce McCandless replied—

"Roger, 11, we're recording your comments for posterity."

Armstrong, Edwin Aldrin and Michael Collins checked that all items were functioning properly during last night's parking orbit.

Armstrong and Aldrin fly to the moon surface today in the four-legged lunar module.

Collins will cross at two points on his side of the moon.

Professor John Davies reported at Jodrell Bank that the chances

MOON BABY

...nd Mrs Jack Robertson, of ...ilton Park, Monifieth, are ...their son Neil Edwin ...fter the three astronauts, ...born 13 minutes after ...lifted off from Cape ...drell Bank...
...Wednesday.

£16,500 FOR CH...

of a collision were "negligible, and far less than a collision with a meteorite."

ALL-NIGHT TV

B.B.C. and ITV are not closing down tonight.

When Armstrong is about to set foot on the moon an alarm clock will ring on ITV for viewers who have nodded off.

Twenty South Africans flew into London yesterday to watch the landing on a hotel television set.

They spent £250 each on the 12,000-mile return trip.

South Africa has no TV.

MISS BARBARA INNOCENT, 31 Wallfield Crescent, Aberdeen, married Mr Robert Jones, son of Professor and Mrs R. V. Jones, 8 King's College, Aberdeen, in King's College Chapel, Aberdeen, yesterday.

The bride has just graduated in psychology, with honours, from Aberdeen University, and her husband is a geophysicist in Edinburgh. Attending the bride were sisters Rosemary Jones (left) and Mrs Susan Parente, a former Miss Scotland, and now residing in America. The couple are to make their home in New Guinea.

Edward Kennedy Escapes In Car Plunge

SENATOR EDWARD KENNEDY escaped injury yesterday, but a woman passenger drowned when the car he was driving plunged into the sea.

Police Chief Dominic Arena said they were the only passengers in the vehicle, which went into the water by a bridge connecting Martha's Vineyard and Chappaquiddick Island, Massachusetts.

FAIRFAX CROSSES ATLANTIC —AFTER 180 DA...

BRITISH oarsman John Fairfax pac... Hollywood Beach, Florida, th... Atlantic Ocean alone.

The epic 180-day journey covered...

Earlier, Fairfax had radioed ashore that he could see the hotels at Miami Beach.

"I've had enough and I'm coming in," he radioed friend Kenneth Crutchlow at Fort Lauderdale.

"Can you give me a phone number where I can reach you?"

Two boats, one carrying a party of the oarsman's friends and a second a contingent of newsmen, headed south from Fort Lauderdale to rendezvous with him.

Then Fairfax was spotted by a Miami yachtsman, Dr Leonard Maceiras, who cruised abeam of the 24-foot rowboat.

"I'm in good shape, but I'm going to rest up before rowing on. I'm gasping for a smoke," he told Dr Maceiras, who tossed him a package of cigarettes.

Hundreds of week...
into the...

19 Children Drowned: Camp Director Charged

M. MICHEL DELAUNAY, the director of a children's summer camp, was charged at Angers, France, yesterday with causing death through negligence following the drowning of 19 children from the camp.

M. Delaunay (27), who was re-manded in custody, led the party on a picnic outing on the banks of the River Loire which ended in tragedy.

Twenty-three children were swept into the fast-flowing river when they waded out to a sandbank which collapsed under them.

Four children were rescued by a fisherman in a boat.

All the children who died were aged between 11 and 14.

Five Out Of Six F...

...ro...ped to Britain ...incident claiming four ...Frenchmen were injured.

OOR WULLIE 1960-1969

The Sunday Post 26th June 1960

OOR WULLIE 1960-1969

The Sunday Post 6th May 1962

The Sunday Post 13th November 1966

OOR WULLIE 1960-1969

The Sunday Post 28th August 1960

OOR WULLIE 1960-1969

The Sunday Post 23rd June 1968

The Sunday Post 24th September 1961

OOR WULLIE 1960-1969

The Sunday Post 17th November 1968

The Sunday Post 10th July 1966

The Sunday Post 4th February 1968

The Sunday Post 5th February 1995

The Sunday Post 25th June 1995

The Sunday Post 17th September 1995

The Sunday Post 10th December 1995

OOR WULLIE

For a period after the death of Dudley D. Watkins, strips previously published were reprinted during the 70's, while the editorial team looked for a replacement artist to take on the daunting task of producing two pages per week. Several artists were used during this period.

Current illustrator Ken H. Harrison has shouldered the onerous task of drawing Oor Wullie and The Broons manfully since November 1989. His work is reproduced here.